The Nutcracker

Written by
Susan Chandler

Illustrated by
Kate Leake

Albury Children's

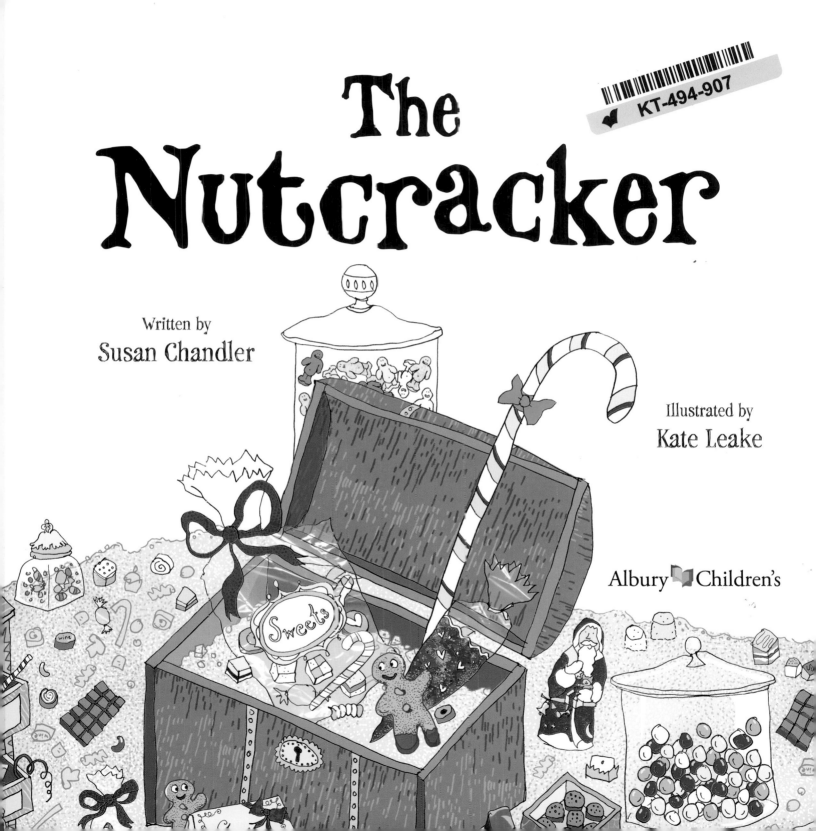

There were **no** sweets.

No fruit chews or lollipops,
no Turkish delight, no cherry drops.
No cough candy or chocolate fudge,
no lemon sherberts or mint humbugs.

'When I was a girl,' Frau Stalbaum began, 'there were sweets everywhere, there were even sweet shops!' The children stared at their mother in disbelief.

'Now hurry up, Fritz,' she said.
'You'll be late for the party.'

Fritz buttoned his jacket and Clara pulled on her party shoes.
'Where have all the sweets gone?' Clara asked.

'Well I have a theory,' whispered their
mother mysteriously.
'I think the Mouse King stole them.'

Their eyes widened.

'They say he has magic powers,'
Frau Stalbaum continued.
'They say he turned a boy into a nutcracker doll.'

'That's a rubbish story!' declared Fritz rudely.
'I'm going down to the party now.'

'You too, Clara,' said her mother
smiling at her own mischief.

Dr Stalbaum was already making a toast when Fritz and Clara arrived.

'This Christmas Eve
we have such a treat in store!
All the toymakers have come with
a present for every single child
here tonight!'

The children scurried about excitedly.
Fritz had spotted a bright green train
and made sure he got there first.
Clara looked carefully about her
and saw that one toymaker
had brought with him a nutcracker doll.

'May I have this toy Herr
Drosselmeyer?' she asked politely.

'Of course you can, Clara,'
said the delighted Toymaker.

The Nutcracker was in her arms for only two minutes when she heard someone hiss...

'Give me that Nutcracker and I'll give you some **chocolate**.'

Chocolate

Clara backed away,
but Fritz had seen the
chocolate from the
other side of the room.

'You can have my engine!' he boomed.
'NO,' replied the woman,
'I want the Nutcracker!'

Clara stepped away clutching the Doll.

'Don't be silly, Clara!'
Fritz said grabbing it from her.

But she held on to it with all
her might. Fritz pulled so hard
that the Nutcracker's arm broke.

The strange lady disappeared.

Clara found Herr Drosselmeyer
just as the party was ending.
'Can you mend him?' she sobbed.

'There there,' he soothed.
'Come tomorrow morning,
he'll be as good as new.'

But Clara could not wait. As she crept downstairs,
she saw the sleeping Toymaker with the Nutcracker
at his side. A shadow was creeping towards them.

'No!'
Clara cried in alarm.

Herr Drosselmeyer awoke with a start.
It was the strange woman again
who let out a furious squeak.

She threw off her hat.

There stood the Mouse King baring his teeth!

'What are you staring at?' he growled.

The Nutcracker slowly opened
his wooden mouth and replied,

**'You! You
puffed up
fur-ball!'**

Suddenly,
a thousand mice poured into the hall.
The Nutcracker turned to look. As he did so
the Mouse King knocked him down with his sword.

'Now you're for it!'
the Mouse King laughed.

The Mouse King got ready
to attack the Nutcracker.

Clara thought very quickly.
She took off her slippers
and threw them at him.

The Mouse King dropped
his sword and the
Nutcracker seized his
chance and stabbed the
King through the heart.

A magical mist
encircled the Nutcracker.

'Look, Clara!'
Drosselmeyer said.

'He's turning back into my
nephew! Hans-Peter!'

Hans-Peter
jumped to his feet.

'We must follow the mice!'
he cried. 'They will be taking
him to their secret hideaway.
We must go now!'

The boy ran off
after the mouse procession.

Clara and the Toymaker followed
closely behind. Through the door they went,
hurrying along the silent streets that lead
to the Town Square.

The mice stopped.

Hans-Peter looked at Clara.
'Just you watch,' he said.

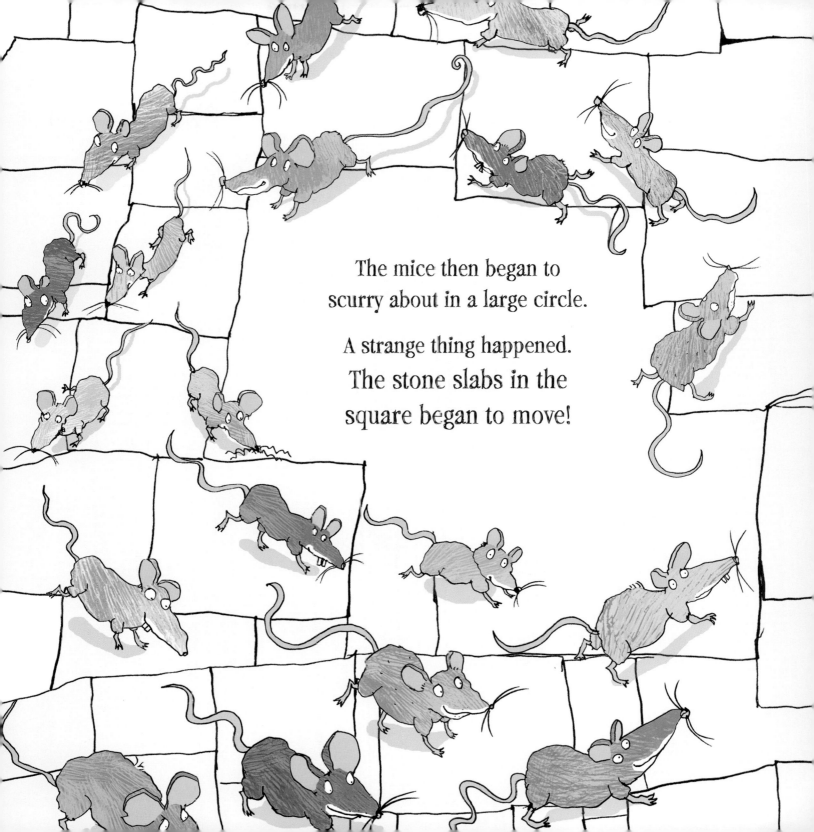

The mice then began to
scurry about in a large circle.

A strange thing happened.
The stone slabs in the
square began to move!

The stones seemed to slide away.

'Take a deep breath,' Hans-Peter told them.
'You won't believe your eyes.'

A delicious beam of light
shone on their faces.

The light grew brighter and
brighter until they could see
a vast cave full of sweets!

There were wine gums and caramels,
chewy toffees and liquorice whirls,
barley sugar and strawberry creams,
aniseed twists and jelly beans.

They shone and twinkled
like precious jewels.

sweets

wine

Sweets

'What is this place?'
asked Herr Drosselmeyer.

'This is the Land of the Sweets,'
came a tiny voice from below.
It was the Sugar Plum Fairy.
She flew out of the cave and over their heads.
'The wicked Mouse King is dead
and we are free,' she trilled.

The Sugar Plum Fairy waved her wand.
The ground began to shake.
The sweets bubbled up from below.

They danced out of the cave
and into the night.
They danced in through letter boxes
and down through chimneys.
Empty shops began to fill up
with delicious candies.

The Sugar Plum Fairy laughed.
'It's time to put some sweetness
back into everybody's life.'

Clara watched with wonder as every
sweet and every chocolate left the cave below.
When the last sweet had gone, the mice
poured in. The stones moved once again
and the cave was re-sealed.

Out in the square, nothing stirred, not even a mouse. Clara picked up a golden toffee from the ground. 'Tomorrow we will play together in the snow,' she beamed at Hans-Peter.

'I'll meet you outside
the Sweet Shop!' he replied.
So the Toymaker and Hans-Peter
took Clara home, and the Sugar
Plum Fairy laughed from above,
delighted to see such a happy ending.

The End

For Charles Elliott
S.C

For orders:
Kuperard Publishers
and Distributors
+44 (0) 208 4462440

First published in 2004
by Meadowside Children's Books,

This edition published by Albury Books in 2013

Albury Court, Albury, Thame, OX9 2LP, United Kingdom

Text © Susan Chandler • Illustrations © Kate Leake
The rights of Susan Chandler and Kate Leake to be identified as the
author and illustrator have been asserted by them in accordance with the
Copyright, Designs and Patents Act, 1988

ISBN 978-1-909958-715 (hardback)
ISBN 978-1-909958-70-8 (paperback)

A CIP Catalogue Record of this title is available from the British Library

Printed in China